Saving the Park

SARAH WILSON

illustrated by Peter Lole

Learning Media

1.
The New Road

I was skateboarding with my friend Maria when I found out about the new road. We were at the park where we meet with our friends every day after school's out. It's just a small park, but it's the only piece of green grass in the whole neighborhood. And it has a skate ramp – a bit worn out, but we don't mind.

That day I'd been trying to do a new move, but I kept falling over. Maria was watching. She isn't scared of falling – when she rides the ramp, it almost looks like she's flying. I knew that she was looking and that I wasn't going to do the right thing.

"I'd better go," I said. I picked up my sweater and tied it around my waist. I saw that the knees of my jeans were nearly worn through. Another reason for Mom to grumble.

"Race you home," called Maria. She tied her hair into a ponytail and whizzed off down Cary Street. I followed right behind her. We're not supposed to skateboard on the sidewalk. People say it's dangerous, and they don't like the noise. But sometimes we do it when there's nobody around.

Maria's quick and tricky, and I couldn't catch her. My hair kept getting in the way, and my eyes stung. Maria looked back to see if I was catching up. "Come on, you turtle!" she laughed.

Then my sweater started falling off my waist, and I had to stop. I leaned up against a store window, and something caught my eye.

"What does this mean?" I said.

"What's up?" called Maria. "Are you OK?"

"Come and look at this," I said.

"You've ruined the race, you skunk. And I was winning," she muttered.

In the store window, there was a handwritten notice. It read, "Stop the new road. Public meeting. Thursday, May 19. Community Hall, 4 p.m."

"Did you know about this?" I asked.

"Yeah. Something about the council wanting to put a new road through here. It's going to join Cary Street with the highway on the other side of the mall."

"But the park!" I said. "Does that mean the new road will go right through the park?"

"Well ... yeah. I suppose so."

I felt ill. Where would we skateboard if the park wasn't there? Lots of kids skateboarded there. A new road would ruin everything.

"Hello! Earth calling Carlos!" I heard Maria saying. "Anyone at home in there?"

"Sorry," I muttered. "I was thinking. We wouldn't be able to skateboard in the park anymore."

"Maybe," she said, "but Mom says the new road will be good. No more traffic jams."

"But what about us?" I asked. "More cars and noise. And no ramp!"

"It's not the end of the world," she said. "Look, I've got to get home. Mom will go crazy if I'm late again. I'll race you." She zoomed off up the street.

I watched Maria disappear around the corner, but I didn't want to chase after her. I stared at the notice for ages. Perhaps if I stared long enough, it would go away.

I usually ride my board all the way home, so I don't notice much. But that day I walked home, dragging my board. I looked at the apartments and the old buildings. Lots of them have been fixed up to look good. A lot of people live here because it's close to the city center. I tried to think of how things would look if a busy road went through.

2.

More Cars, More Noise

"**Y**ou're late," Mom called when I got home. "You were going to help with supper. And do your homework," she added.

"Sorry," I said. "Maria and I were at the park. We kind of forgot the time."

"Wasn't that your excuse yesterday?" she sighed. "And the day before?"

She put our dinner on the table, but I wasn't hungry. I stirred the vegetables around on the plate and made them into different shapes.

"What's wrong, Carlos?" Mom asked. "Did something happen at school today?"

"No. I'm just not hungry."

"I wouldn't be hungry either if my dinner looked like that," she smiled.

I looked down at my dinner and laughed. She was right. What a mess!

"Mom, have you heard about this new road?" I asked.

"Sure. It's going to join Cary Street up with the highway to Glenville. The council says there are so many cars coming into the city they need a bigger road. I thought you knew about it."

"No! Nobody tells me anything," I moaned.

"That's because you never listen. You spend so much time on that skateboard."

"There's a meeting about it on Thursday," I said. "I might go."

I went to bed early, but I couldn't sleep. It was too hot, and street sounds floated up through the open window – traffic noise, people talking, doors banging. My curtains don't close tight, and the streetlight always shines in. I got up and looked outside. I could see our neighbor, Jack, sitting outside. Perhaps he'd know what to do about the new road.

I pulled on my jeans and an old sweater and crept down the hall. I carefully opened the door, and crossed the road to see Jack.

"Hi, Jack!" I said.

"Hello, boy," Jack smiled at me.

"Do you know anything about this new road – the one that's going through here?" I asked.

"Sure do. Some of us have been trying to stop it," he said.

"Why didn't anyone tell me about it?" I asked.

"Well, if you spent less time on that skateboard of yours …"

I groaned. I've heard that too many times lately. "But there must be a lot of people around here who don't want a new road," I said.

"Well, I tried, and I didn't get anywhere. The council doesn't seem to listen to the folk who live and work round here, anyway," Jack said.

"What do you think will happen?" I asked.

"Well, a new road will mean more cars. If people think they can get across town quicker, they'll stop using buses and trains. There'll be lots more noise and gas fumes. And all those cars whizzing about ...."

Suddenly I heard Mom calling. "Carlos, get back to bed. Do you know what time it is? You should have been asleep hours ago!"

"Good luck to you," said Jack, and he went back to watching the street.

3.

A Bright Idea

That night, I had really weird dreams – huge machines pushing dirt about, people shouting, and skateboarders everywhere. I woke up really early and couldn't get back to sleep – I felt like I'd had no sleep at all.

I didn't say much at breakfast, but Mom didn't seem to notice. She hadn't even noticed that I was up early. I grabbed my board and headed off to school.

"Carlos!" she called after me. "Don't ride on the sidewalk."

"Sure," I yelled back. She said the same thing every day.

I walked along the street toward school. As I turned the corner, I saw Frankie and Maria up ahead.

"Wait up, guys," I called.

"You're out of bed early. Are you OK? Not sick, are you?" Frankie joked.

"I couldn't sleep, wise guy! I kept on thinking about this stupid road," I said.

"What road?" Frankie asked.

"The one that's going smack through the middle of the park. There'll be no more skateboarding for us! There must be something we can do."

"*We* can do!" said Maria. "Who'd listen to us?"

"We'll never know unless we try," I said. "And if everyone thought that way, nothing would ever get done, would it?"

When I got to the school gates, Miss James, our teacher, was riding her bike into the grounds. She's the only teacher who doesn't drive a car to school, so I wasn't surprised to find out that she knew a lot about the road. She was even in a protest group that wanted to stop the council going ahead with their plans. She was surprised when I said *I* wanted to help. I guess I'm not usually into that kind of thing.

"If the road goes ahead, we won't be able to skateboard. The nearest park is miles away," I said.

"So that's why you're interested," she smiled. "Well, why don't you bring some of your friends to the meeting. We need as many people there as possible."

After school, I went straight to the park to wait for Maria and Frankie. Some other kids were already there, boarding on the curbs and rails and doing tricks on the ramp. I watched my friend Pete try a handplant.

"Awesome, Pete!" I called.

"Now it's your turn, Carlos," he said.

"Not today. No time," I said. "I've got too much to do." I told him what was happening, and he was really freaked out.

"I'm going to a meeting about it on Thursday," I said.

"You, go to a meeting! No way!" he said.

"Doesn't sound like me, does it? But I'm really angry that some bigwigs think they can just take the park away, and our skate ramp with it. I think that lots of people are worried about having more cars racing about and the pollution – but each of them thinks that nobody else cares. So *they* do nothing, either … see?"

"I think so," said Pete, scratching his head.

"That's why a meeting is such a good idea. People will see that their neighbors are worried too."

"Will there be food there?" he asked, smiling. "Just kidding. OK, I'll come and have a look."

For the rest of the afternoon, I tried to talk to as many kids as I could. I told them we should meet at the park the next day after school. I had an idea.

4.

Twelve Hands

My idea was simple. The only way *I* knew about this whole thing was from reading a notice in a store window. What if we made some huge posters, really bright ones, and put them up all around the neighborhood. Then everyone would know about the meeting.

So the next day after school, Maria and I took some pens and cardboard to the park to make the posters. Frankie and Pete were already there. We waited for a while, and two other kids came along, but that was all. I was disappointed, but twelve hands are better than none. We started working as fast as we could.

By four-thirty we had twenty posters ready, and they looked great. We gathered them up and went home for supper. I dumped them on the kitchen counter and started to pick at the salad Mom was making. "Don't do that, you pest," she said, "and what's all this mess? Clear it away so I have some room to move here."

"It's not mess," I said. "It's all of our work from this afternoon. They're posters to tell people about the meeting next Thursday."

Mom looked worried when I told her what we were doing. "Carlos, it's great you want to stop this road, but don't get your hopes up. It's sometimes hard to get people to work together or to change their minds about things like this."

"I know, but it won't feel right if we don't try," I said. "It's really important. Ask Miss James about it at the meeting."

"Well, Thursday's a busy day for me, Carlos. You know I take Mrs. Mendez grocery shopping, and I'm minding Carla so her mom can have a bit of time to herself …."

"I don't believe this," I said. "You're always telling me to forget skateboarding and find something else to do. Now when I do try to do something useful, you'd … you'd rather go shopping than come along and see what it's all about?"

"It's not like that, Carlos, and you know it," she said. "Mrs. Mendez needs help. She's not well."

I said, "I guess so." But I felt let down. I thought Mom would be pleased about what I was doing.

Over the next few days, we went around stores and asked if we could put our posters in the windows. Only one guy said no, so we kept that one to take to the meeting.

5.

The Big Day

On the Thursday of the meeting, time really dragged at school, and I was jittery all day. Miss James got mad at me because I wasn't doing much work. But finally the bell rang, and Maria and I made our way to the park. We waited for Pete and Frankie to get there, and we walked across to the hall together. When we got there, people were standing everywhere outside and the hall was packed. We were the only kids, and everyone looked surprised to see us. We squeezed our way inside and stood against a wall. Miss James was sitting at a table at the front. She waved and gave the thumbs-up when she saw our sign. Then I saw Mom. She was sitting in the front row, bouncing little Carla on her knee. That made me feel even better.

The meeting began, and there was lots of yelling and whistling. Some people were really angry, and their voices got louder and louder. Mr. Frank said the new road would go through his video store and he would have to close. He'd lived and worked around here for years. Where would he go? Someone said that people should ride the buses and trains to work instead of driving their cars. Someone else said that they liked driving to work, but the crowd didn't like that at all.

The meeting went on and on and seemed to be getting nowhere. I was getting hot and tired. Pete and Maria were wriggling in their seats and whispering.

"Shhhh," I said.

"When's this going to be over?" Pete asked.

"Soon," I said. "Just wait a while."

Then Miss James stood up. "It's getting late," she said. "Next week, there's going to be a council meeting to decide on the new road, so we have to let them know how we feel. We need to show the council that we're not happy – not just one or two of us, but everyone. We need everyone to write down what they think and send it in so that the mayor and the council can read it. Or you could telephone the council during the day. Before we go, I'd like to thank Carlos and his friends for their hard work. The posters look great. We've had a great turnout at this meeting, and you guys helped a lot!"

As we were leaving, Miss James came over. "Well done, you guys. You're all regular artists," she said. "We could use some help with flyers, if you have the time. We need someone to do the fancy lettering, and they need to be delivered to the whole neighborhood too."

I looked at my friends. They were looking down at their feet.

"Come on, guys," I said. "They don't have to be works of art. You saw how many people came along today. We helped to do that. We can save the park and the ramp."

They nodded. "Yeah, OK," said Pete. "I guess we can try."

6.
A New Ramp

In the weeks before the big meeting, we did a lot of work. We made flyers and put them in mailboxes. Miss James came down to the park and helped us pass out some flyers there. She hadn't realized how run-down the place was. "Perhaps if the road doesn't go through, we can fix this up … maybe build a new ramp," she said.

Miss James took leave the next week while the council meeting was on. We had another teacher called Mr. Lynch who made us work really hard. Maria and I were glad when Miss James walked back into the room at the end of class on Friday.

"It's great to be back," she said. "It's been a really hard week." She looked really tired, and my heart took a dive. "But I've got some news," she said. "Some good news, Carlos. The new road isn't going through this year. The council's given the community until next year to think of other ways to fix the traffic problem. They had so many letters and telephone calls after that meeting, it made them sit up and think! We haven't won yet – we still have some work to do – but it's great news."

Maria and I jumped about, yelling and clowning around with our boards. We were so happy. Suddenly our principal, Mrs. Fernandez, came in. She was really mad. "What on earth is going on here?" she demanded.

"I'm sorry about the noise, Mrs. Fernandez. It's just that we've had some good news, and we were celebrating," said Miss James.

"That's all very fine," said Mrs. Fernandez, "but keep the noise down. And put that skateboard down, Carlos," she said, glaring at me. We waited for her to leave, and then Miss James said, "Come on, kids. The burgers are on me!"

That evening, there was a party at the hall. We were hanging out at the back talking when Miss James and the guy from the skateboard store came over.

"This is Sid. He wants to help you fix up the ramp," she said.

"Tomorrow we'll start by making it safe," Sid told us. "Then, if we manage to stop this road for good, we can think about building a new, bigger ramp."

That sounded good to me. It all sounded good, and it felt good to be part of it.

We walked home past the park and hung out there for a while. People were out walking and kids were running around. I looked at the ramp. Maybe I'd try some new moves after we fixed it up tomorrow – even if Maria *was* watching.